Elspeth Hart
and the
Perilous Voyage

For Ellen and Kirsty, with love – SF
For Mum and Dad x – JB

STRIPES PUBLISHING
An imprint of Little Tiger Press
1 The Coda Centre, 189 Munster Road,
London SW6 6AW

A paperback original
First published in Great Britain in 2015

Text copyright © Sarah Forbes, 2015
Illustrations copyright © James Brown, 2015
Background images courtesy of www.shutterstock.com

ISBN: 978-1-84715-608-2

A CIP catalogue record for this book is available from the British Library.

Printed and bound in the UK.

10 9 8 7 6 5 4 3 2 1

Elspeth Hart
and the
Perilous Voyage

Sarah Forbes

Illustrated by James Brown

Stripes

Prologue

If you met Elspeth Hart, dear reader, you wouldn't think there was anything unusual about her. In fact, you would think she was quite ordinary. Elspeth was ten years old. She was a bit shorter than you are and a bit shyer than you are. She had long dark hair that never looked neat, no matter how much she brushed it.

But Elspeth Hart's world was *most* unusual. She had just escaped from two kidnappers called Miss Crabb and Gladys Goulash, who had been keeping her captive in the dreadful Pandora Pants School for Show-offs.

Why had Miss Crabb and Gladys Goulash kidnapped Elspeth, I hear you ask? Well, Elspeth's parents owned a little sweet shop and they had come up with a marvellous secret recipe for the most delicious toffee sauce in the world. Now Miss Crabb was a mean, greedy woman and she wanted to get her hands on this recipe. She wanted it more than anything, dear reader. She wanted it more than you might want a day off school or a big plate of chips for your dinner. Miss Crabb was convinced she could make millions selling the Extra-special

Sticky Toffee Sauce.

But Miss Crabb hadn't managed to get hold of Elspeth's family recipe, because Elspeth had kept it safe. And Elspeth had even come up with a clever plan to run away, leaving Miss Crabb and her sidekick Gladys Goulash to be locked up in jail.

Elspeth had made it all the way from the Pandora Pants School for Show-offs back to her home, which was a little flat above her parents' sweet shop. But when she got there, she found the shop and the flat dark and empty. There was no sign of Elspeth's parents, only a note explaining that they had gone searching for her. The note said Elspeth should go straight to the police, but just before she reached the police station, she spotted a newspaper and read some very bad news indeed…

EVIL DINNER LADIES IN DARING ESCAPE!

A nationwide search has started after two dastardly dinner ladies, Miss Crabb and Gladys Goulash, went missing from Grimguts high-security prison yesterday. It is thought that the dinner ladies, arrested for a treacherous kidnapping and fraud plot, may have escaped by hiding in large bags of dirty laundry.

Members of the public are advised not to approach them, as they are highly dangerous and smell awful.

1
The Awful Newspaper Headline

Elspeth stared at the newspaper headline
in horror.

"Miss Crabb and Gladys Goulash have
escaped!" she said. She whirled around and
started sprinting back towards her house.
Elspeth knew that the first thing Miss
Crabb and Gladys Goulash would do was
come looking for her parents' precious

Extra-special Sticky Toffee Sauce recipe.

Elspeth burst through the gate and raced up the steps to her front door, fumbling for her key. She shoved the key in the lock, threw open the door and rushed inside.

And then it hit her. A dreadful and familiar smell.

"Oh no," Elspeth said under her breath. "No, no, no!"

There was only one person in the world who smelled that bad – Gladys Goulash, who hated washing and only had a bath once a year. As Elspeth ran into the living room, she discovered a trail of destruction – muddy footprints, upturned chairs, books scattered on the floor. It had to be the work of Miss Crabb.

Elspeth Hart paused. Where had she left the precious recipe? Her mind went blank for a second, then it came to her. She had put it on the mantelpiece. Elspeth ran over and looked around wildly.

Hart's Extra-special Sticky Toffee Sauce Recipe, the one her parents had tried so hard to protect … was gone.

Miss Crabb and Gladys Goulash had got what they wanted at last.

"How could I have been so *stupid*?" Elspeth cried. "I should never have let the recipe out of my sight!" The recipe was so top secret that her parents had made up a special code for the ingredients. Her mum and dad had gone to all that trouble to keep the recipe safe and now that it was gone, Elspeth felt quite lost and awfully guilty.

Elspeth gazed down at the scribbles on her trainers, feeling miserable. She trudged through the flat, looking at the chaos Miss Crabb and Gladys Goulash had caused. The kitchen window had been smashed and it looked like they'd used a ladder to climb up and get inside. In Elspeth's room, the sheets on her bed were messed up, and her parents' bedroom had been turned upside down. Miss Crabb and Gladys Goulash had raided the cupboards and ransacked the bathroom. They had been *everywhere.*

Elspeth stared at the mess and bit by bit, she didn't feel so sad. She felt very, very vexed. I imagine you know, dear reader, that when someone does something horrible to you, you might feel sad at first. But then you might feel angry. And Elspeth was angry now.

"Right," she said out loud. "If you two reckon you can get away with stealing my mum and dad's top-secret recipe, you're wrong."

Elspeth went back into the kitchen, moving slowly this time, hunting for clues.

On the windowsill she spotted something. It was the same newspaper

Elspeth had seen earlier, with the headline about Crabb and Goulash's escape, but now it was lying open at an article about a fancy cruise ship. And it had notes scrawled all over it in Miss Crabb's handwriting.

HMS UNSINKABLE

THE maiden voyage of the record-breakingly posh new cruise liner, the *HMS Unsinkable*, is set to stun the world. The *HMS Unsinkable* carries 8,000 passengers and will set sail from Southampton to New York on Thursday 12th July at 6 p.m. Several celebrities and members of the aristocracy will be on board, including the country's richest couple, Lord and Lady Spewitt, and the famous explorer, Baron Van Der Blink. It is thought that the boat will set new standards in luxury travel – Poppy and Pippy Delamere, hairdressers and beauty therapists for the royal family, have been booked to work in a luxury salon on board. Tickets have been sold at around £50,000 one way. Read on for details of the *HMS Unsinkable*'s most glamorous guests...

Oooh, lovely!

Nobody will catch us in America!

Get rid of those hair and beauty ladies and take their places!

Miss Crabb and Gladys Goulash had been in such a rush that they had left something *very* interesting behind.

Elspeth's eyes widened as she read.

SETS SAIL

She looked up from the newspaper.

"So you're heading to America? And you think nobody will catch you, Miss Crabb?" Elspeth muttered. "Think again. I'm getting that recipe back."

The article said that the cruise ship was leaving on Thursday. Elspeth Hart had ONE DAY.

2
One Very Important Day

Miss Crabb and Gladys Goulash were hurrying away from Elspeth's house at top speed in a stolen car, planning how to get on board the *HMS Unsinkable*. They had done a lot of bad things in their time, from making soups full of toenail clippings to kidnapping Elspeth Hart, but this was one of their nastiest plans yet.

"Hah!" said Miss Crabb, as they zoomed on to the motorway. "A luxury trip to New York on the *HMS Unsinkable*. Won't that be lovely! And when we get to America, we can start making the Extra-special Sticky Toffee Sauce and selling it for loads of money." She shoved the recipe down the front of her jumper to keep it safe.

"Ooh, New York," said Gladys Goulash. "Is that near York?"

Gladys Goulash was very stupid. Miss Crabb only kept her around to do all her dirty work.

"No, you fool! It's in America — that's a completely different country." Miss Crabb smiled, showing her grimy false teeth. "Just the right place to set up our top-secret Extra-special Sticky Toffee Sauce factory. We'll make millions, Gladys Goulash!"

Gladys sniffed. "Why can't we just fly there? Much quicker that way," she said.

Miss Crabb stamped her foot in rage, accidentally hitting the accelerator and making the car lurch forward. "You KNOW we've been banned from flying ever since we started a fight on the plane back from our holiday in Spain," she said.

"Oh yeah," Gladys said. "The one where we tried to take that donkey home with us!"

"And in case you have forgotten, you blithering doughnut, we're ON THE RUN!"

Miss Crabb continued. "That means the police will nab us if we try to leave the country."

"Well then," said Gladys Goulash, "they're not gonna let us get on a big posh boat, are they?"

"Gah!" Miss Crabb was losing her temper. But then she remembered how useful Gladys Goulash would be for doing all the hard work in her Extra-special Sticky Toffee Sauce factory while Miss Crabb lay around eating biscuits and having naps. She would have to put up with her dim-witted friend for a bit longer.

"We're not going to buy tickets," she said crossly. "We're going to go on *in disguise*. We're going to pretend to be the ladies who run the hair and beauty salon on the *HMS Unsinkable*. We'll buy wigs so nobody can recognize us, then we'll bluff our way on board. If that doesn't work, I'll shove my way on – I have very sharp elbows. And then we'll lock the real hair and beauty ladies up in a cupboard and take their place! Eee-hee-hee!" Miss Crabb sat back, looking extremely smug.

Elspeth raced to the train station, carrying a rucksack stuffed with some clothes and the newspaper Miss Crabb and Gladys Goulash had left behind. She knew she'd need help if she was going to get the better of Miss Crabb and Gladys Goulash, and there was only one person she could trust – her best friend, Rory Snitter. Rory had been Elspeth's only friend when she was forced to live in the Pandora Pants School for

Show-offs. The other students at the school hadn't cared about Elspeth at all.

Elspeth knew where Rory lived, but she had no money to buy a train ticket. She paused at the station entrance to catch her breath and thought hard.

The station was packed full of people rushing to catch trains, pushing into queues and drinking cups of coffee. Elspeth was glad it was busy – it meant she could slip in between the grown-ups without being noticed. There was a train to Rory's village leaving in five minutes, so Elspeth headed towards the platform, hoping she might be able to talk her way on board without a ticket, but there were barriers in the way.

"Excuse me, please can I get on the train? My mum's on it already. She's got our tickets," Elspeth said to a ticket inspector.

She crossed her fingers behind her back.

"A likely tale," said the ticket inspector. He scowled down at Elspeth. "I've had enough of kids like you mucking about. Summer holidays start and this place is over-run. I ought to report you!"

Elspeth's eyes widened. "Please don't report me," she squeaked. "I'll go home at once. Sorry!" Elspeth scurried away as fast as she could. But she didn't go home. Elspeth Hart didn't give up that easily. She hid behind a coffee stall and waited.

From her hiding place she could see that people were lifting bikes and big suitcases into the luggage carriage at the very end of the train. If Elspeth could just sneak in there, she wouldn't need a ticket at all. But she still had to get through those barriers.

"Unless…" she said to herself.

Elspeth waited until the ticket inspector was busy helping someone else, then she followed a man with a bike who was striding towards the barriers. As soon as the gate opened to let him through, Elspeth hurried behind and followed him towards the luggage carriage, trying to look casual. She was desperate to make a run for it, but that would only draw attention to her. Once the man had loaded in his bike and turned away, Elspeth leaped into the luggage carriage and hurried to the darkest corner.

"All aboard!" cried the train guard. Elspeth shrank back into the shadows as he peered into the luggage carriage, then the door slammed closed. Elspeth heard the faint sound of the train's whistle and they started to move. They were off.

Elspeth let out a long sigh of relief, then she looked around. It was dark in the luggage carriage, with just a chink of light coming from a high-up window. She found herself a fat suitcase to sit on and leaned her head against the side of the carriage, closing her eyes and letting the rhythm of the train soothe her.

She couldn't stop thinking about her parents and the note they had left her:

Dear, dear Elspeth,

If you find this note, darling girl, you've made it home — that's wonderful. We know someone kidnapped you. We had a mysterious phone call from a woman who wouldn't give her name. She told us you've been stolen and taken to the other side of the world … but we are getting on a plane tonight. We will find you! Go straight to the police and ask them for help.

Mum and Dad xxx

The other side of the world could be *anywhere*. Her parents must have written the note in a hurry, before they had a proper idea of where they were going. Where could they be?

When Elspeth thought about her parents looking for her in some strange place that she had never even been to, she felt very sad and very small.

Then she opened her eyes and told herself to be strong. She would find her parents one day – she *had* to. But for now, she just had one mission – to get that recipe back.

Elspeth *couldn't* let Miss Crabb and Gladys Goulash win.

3
Elspeth
on a Mission

Elspeth climbed down on to the train platform and looked around. Weaseltoe was a quiet station in a peaceful little village. Elspeth could see trees and pretty cottages and even a pond with ducks on it. She slung her rucksack over her shoulder and went right up to the first person she saw – an old man with a walking stick who was tottering along the main road.

"Excuse me," Elspeth said politely. "I'm looking for Snitter Towers. Do you know where it is?"

The old man rolled his eyes. "Oh, I know where it is all right, young lady. You can't miss it," he said. "Just keep following this road. It's a huge white building with a big metal gate. Ridiculous place. That Mrs Snitter's a bit loopy, if you ask me."

Elspeth nodded and hurried on before the old man started asking any questions.

Soon the houses thinned out and Elspeth found herself walking along a tree-lined road. After a few minutes, she spotted high turrets and spires in the distance, and as she came closer, she could see a white building with a tall gate in front of it. The house was absolutely enormous.

If you can imagine a shimmering white castle, dear reader, then you can picture Rory Snitter's house. It was like something from a fairytale. Looking through the railings, Elspeth could see a fountain with a white marble swan on either side of it. There was also a tennis court and a massive swimming pool.

"Wow," breathed Elspeth. She followed a high wall all the way around the house until she found herself back at the big gate. She peeked through again, wondering what to do next.

"I *assume* you have a reason for being on Snitter property?" came a voice from the other side of the gate.

Elspeth jumped. She looked up to see a very tall, pale man in a black suit. He had perfectly neat black hair slicked over to one side and was standing with his hands clasped together in front of him.

"Oh. Yes," Elspeth said. She took a deep breath. "I'm here to see Rory. I'm Elspeth – one of his friends from school."

"Hmmmmm," said the man, peering down at her. He took a monocle from his pocket, popped it in front of his left eye, and stared at her more closely. "I will have to search your bag, young lady. We have security measures here. The property must be protected at all times."

"Of course," Elspeth said nervously. She handed her rucksack through the bars of the gate and the man quickly looked through her things. "Do you … work for Mr and Mrs Snitter?" she asked.

The man breathed in through his nose and stood up very straight. "I do," he said.

"I am Mr Tunnock, the butler. I am in charge of the house and grounds – and I'm also in charge of Master Rory, as his parents are not here." Mr Tunnock flicked a tiny bit of dust from his jacket. "I am proud to say I have served this family for over eighteen years."

He handed Elspeth her rucksack. "Very well," he said, punching a code into the metal gate. "You may enter."

The gate creaked open and Elspeth went inside. As they made their way down the long drive, past the fountain, she spotted a small figure.

"Rory!" Elspeth yelled.

Rory stopped and stared. Then he dropped the tennis racket he was carrying, ran towards Elspeth and gave her a huge hug.

"Elspeth! What are you doing here?" he cried.

Elspeth stepped back and smiled at her friend. Rory was dressed in perfectly ironed tennis whites and looked very smart, except for a tuft of hair that was sticking up crazily, like always.

His pet lizard, Lazlo, was sitting on his shoulder and looking at her curiously.

"I've got SO MUCH to tell you!" Elspeth said. She glanced round to see Mr Tunnock standing a couple of metres away, watching her carefully.

"Mr Tunnock let me in. He said your parents are away?"

"Yes, they're on one of their long holidays," Rory said. "Two whole months!" He turned to the butler. "Don't worry, Tunners, Elspeth won't be any trouble."

Mr Tunnock gave a low bow and turned back to the fountain. He took a silk handkerchief from his pocket and started polishing one of the marble swans.

"Are you OK?" Rory asked, taking Elspeth's rucksack and heading towards the house. "Tell me everything!"

Elspeth gazed around as they walked along a path with grand columns on either side. They went through a set of giant oak doors with enormous bolts on them, and into a vast hallway filled with ornaments, flower displays, paintings and another fountain. Rory's house was the grandest place Elspeth had ever seen.

"I know, I know," Rory said when he noticed her staring. "It's a bit over the top, isn't it? Come on, we'll sit in the kitchen."

They sat down at the huge kitchen table and Rory poured them both a glass of juice.

"So," Rory said, "last time I saw you, you were running away from school as fast as you could. Mr Tunnock picked me up just after you left and brought me straight home. I hope I never see that horrible school ever again. Lazlo's much happier now we're back. Did you ever find your parents' secret sticky toffee sauce recipe? You said you thought the ingredients were in that song you remembered."

"Yes, I did! They were in my head all along," Elspeth said. "But the amounts – you know, how many spoons of syrup and that kind of thing … were written on my trainers!" She lifted up her foot so Rory could see the tiny numbers that her dad had hidden among the doodles on her

shoes. "So when I wrote down the ingredients AND the numbers and put it all together, I had the recipe after all!"

"Wow!" Rory said, and Lazlo jumped on to Elspeth's knee to take a look.

"But that's just the start of it," Elspeth said. "I got all the way home … and the house was empty. Mum and Dad had left me a note – they've gone abroad to try and find me. Some woman phoned them and told them I'd left the country! But their note didn't say exactly where they were going."

"Hmmm," Rory frowned. "I bet that was Miss Crabb who called them, trying to get your parents out of the way."

"Yes, I think so, too." Elspeth nodded. "I was on my way to the police station this morning to get help, when I saw this."

She unrolled the newspaper from her bag and laid it on the table, showing the headline:

EVIL DINNER LADIES IN DARING ESCAPE!

Rory went pale. Lazlo sensed something was wrong, too. He ran down Rory's arm and started biting the edge of the newspaper.

"It gets even worse," Elspeth said. Rory and Lazlo both stared at her, listening carefully. "Miss Crabb and Gladys Goulash broke into my house," Elspeth explained. "They got in this morning and stole the recipe for the Extra-special Sticky Toffee Sauce!"

"WHAT?" Rory went even paler.

"Yes," Elspeth said. "I need to find them, so I can get it back."

4

The Plan to Get the Recipe Back

"Elspeth, you can't! It's too dangerous!"
Rory said. "You can just put another copy
of the recipe together, can't you? You know
the code now… Why would you go chasing
after them?"

"Think about it," Elspeth said. "The most
important thing is that there is only ever
one copy of that recipe! Hart's Extra-special

Sticky Toffee Sauce won't be so extra special if Crabb and Goulash know how to make it! I've GOT to get it back. I'm going after them."

"Elspeth," Rory said earnestly. "I think you need to stay as far away from those two as possible. You'll be safe here. We've got electronic gates and security cameras and everything."

Elspeth wasn't a bossy person, but she could be very determined sometimes.

"Rory, you know how important that recipe is to my mum and dad. And it's my fault that Crabb and Goulash got their hands on it, so I have to get it back. I know exactly where we have to go to find it." She flicked through the newspaper and showed Rory the article about the *HMS Unsinkable.*

Rory started to read, looking nervous.

Elspeth pointed to Miss Crabb's scribbles. "See? They're going to get on the ship pretending to be the ladies who work in the hair and beauty salon. We have to get on the ship, too!"

Rory was much more cautious than Elspeth. From the look on his face, she could see that he'd need a bit of persuading.

"Please, Rory. You're the only one I can trust. Plus … it'll be an adventure!" Elspeth gave him her most pleading look. "We need to go straight away, though. The ship sails tomorrow."

Rory stared at her. "You can't be serious," he said.

"I am! We'll need money for the train, then we just have to get on board the ship somehow," Elspeth said.

"You want to sneak on to a ship ... that's going all the way to America ... in case that ship has Miss Crabb on it? Are you insane?"

Lazlo hopped up and down on Rory's shoulder.

Elspeth nodded firmly. "I'm getting on that boat, Rory. It's my only chance! I'll go on my own if I have to, but I'd really like you to come with me. Together I *know* we can get the better of Miss Crabb and Gladys Goulash. Please? *Pleeeeeease?*"

Elspeth knew she'd persuaded Rory when she saw a tiny smile appear on his face.

"OK, OK, OK," said Rory, "I'll come – I can't let you do this alone. Even though I think it's a mad idea."

"Rory! Thank you!" Elspeth gave him a hug and he blushed. Then she sat down and pulled her notebook out of her rucksack.

"Right, it said in the paper that the ship sails at six o'clock tomorrow evening. It'll be hard to sneak off without Mr Tunnock noticing. Maybe we should slip away tonight, when he's asleep."

"I don't think that's a good idea," said Rory. "He'd realize I was gone in the morning. Then he'd have to phone my mum and dad to say I'm missing."

"Hmm." Elspeth thought for a minute. "You need an excuse to go away for a bit. That way, Mr Tunnock won't be worried about you, and your parents will never know you've been gone. Hey, couldn't we say we're off to a summer camp? Like … a tap-dancing camp!"

"Perfect!" Rory's eyes lit up. "Tunners knows I wasn't getting good marks in Tap last year. Yes, we'll tell him we're going to tap-dancing camp in Southampton."

"I know… Let's write a VERY convincing note," Elspeth said.

"Yes!" said Rory. "Good idea, Elspeth. Follow me." They dashed down the hall and into Mrs Snitter's study.

Rory grabbed a fountain pen, a sheet of writing paper and a handwritten to-do list that was sitting next to the phone:

Snitter Towers

Tell Tunnock to clean my diamond collection

Tell Tunnock to buy a large box of caviar

Tell Tunnock to buy another ornamental swan for the fountain

Tell Tunnock to invite the Duke and Duchess of Hiccupingshire to tea

Very carefully, copying his mum's handwriting, Rory wrote a note:

> Tunnock,
>
> Rory and his school friend Elspeth shall be attending tap-dancing camp in Southampton beginning on 12th July.
>   Do be a darling and drive them down there, won't you?

Rory paused for a minute, chewing the end of the pen and thinking.

"One more thing," said Elspeth. "We might need some food."

Rory nodded. "Yes. We'll need plenty of chocolate for Lazlo, too. It's the only thing that keeps him quiet."

He started writing again.

You might also provide them with some tasty sandwiches and chocolate bars, as the food in these places is quite dreadful.

"That's the sort of thing she would say," Rory said. Then he added a big squiggly signature. "Now what?" he asked.

"Now we give Mr Tunnock the note and tell him to be ready to set out straight after lunch tomorrow," said Elspeth.

5

Straight After Lunch
the Next Day

Rory and Elspeth climbed out of the car
at Southampton docks. When they had
given Mr Tunnock the note that morning,
he had simply read it, nodded slowly and
gone to make their sandwiches. After
lunch, they'd climbed into the family
limousine and Mr Tunnock had driven
them all the way to Southampton in

silence. But he did look slightly suspicious now they had arrived.

"I trust you have all you need?" he asked. Elspeth had her rucksack and Rory had a satchel with him. Mr Tunnock looked around the docks. "Where are the other children?"

"Don't worry, they won't be far away. This is definitely the meeting place," Elspeth said confidently.

"Yes, thanks Tunners," Rory added. "No offence, but it's not cool to be seen with the grown-up who dropped you off. We'd rather go and find everyone by ourselves, if that's OK."

Mr Tunnock nodded and gave them a solemn wave as he started the car.

As soon as he had driven off, Elspeth and Rory turned and gazed up at the vast bulk of the *HMS Unsinkable*.

It was white and shiny, as long as three football pitches and even taller than Rory Snitter's house. I'm sure you can imagine, dear reader, how very tiny Elspeth and Rory felt as they stared up at the majestic ship sitting in the dock. There were people everywhere, waving from the deck and saying tearful goodbyes. A man on the gangway was checking tickets as people boarded.

"Elspeth, how are we going to get on board without being seen?" Rory asked, tucking Lazlo into his shirt pocket.

Elspeth had been wondering the same thing. But before she could reply, a stretch limousine squealed to a halt beside them, making them both leap out of the way.

"We're late, Albert! We really are frightfully frightfully late!" shrieked a large woman in a tweed suit, flinging herself out of the car. "They'll sail without us and we'll miss our best chance of becoming friends with Lord and Lady Spewitt! Oh dear, oh dear, oh dear!"

"Yes, yes, Petunia," said a tired-looking

man, following her towards the ship. He waved at the porters. "I say, you there! Bring our trunks in, will you? Cabin 12A and be quick about it."

The couple hurried up the gangway as a porter hauled their luggage out of the limo.

Elspeth stared in astonishment. They were the biggest trunks she had ever seen. *Wait a minute…* she thought. *You could fit a grown man in there!*

She grabbed Rory's hand and started to run. As soon as the porter was looking away, Elspeth opened the biggest trunk and clambered inside, pulling Rory in after her and letting the lid close softly.

There was a horrible smell of mothballs, but a small crack in the side of the trunk meant they had a little light and just enough air. Elspeth dragged a heavy ballgown over their heads.

"Just stay very still," she whispered.

"Easy for you to say," said Rory. "Lazlo hates being cooped up – you know that." Rory squirmed to the side a bit and dug a piece of chocolate out of his pocket. "This'll keep him quiet for a minute or two, but it won't be long before he starts biting."

There was muffled thumping outside. Elspeth held her breath as the trunk was lifted up. Then, judging by the slow, jerky movements, it felt like they were being carried aboard.

"Weighs a flipping ton, this does," said one of the porters. "What's she got in here, solid gold?"

"Wouldn't be surprised," said the other. "Hope she tips us!"

Thud-drag, thud-drag, thud-drag.

"At least those two passengers aren't as bad as the women getting on earlier," the first porter said. "Did you see them? One's got purple hair and one's got dark hair in a fancy do. They were so bossy with Bill the security guard!"

The second one laughed. "Yeah, they looked like trouble! Bill said they didn't have the right papers, but they work in the hair salon, so he had to let them on. He said the short fat one doesn't smell too good though!"

THUD. Elspeth felt them put the trunk down, then she heard a door bang closed.

"Get out, quick," Elspeth hissed.

They scrambled out.

"Did you hear what those porters were saying?" Elspeth asked in excitement.

"Yes! They must have been talking about Miss Crabb and Gladys Goulash in disguise. You were right – they're on board!" Rory said. He picked up his satchel. "But where should we go first?"

Elspeth looked around. They were in a beautifully furnished cabin with a view out to sea. She could see another door leading to a fancy bathroom. It was all very luxurious, but Elspeth knew they couldn't stay there for long without getting caught.

"I think we should…" Elspeth stopped and put a finger to her lips. She could hear a voice from the corridor and it sounded like the lady they'd seen at the docks.

"Albert, I'm in FRIGHTFUL pain with these new shoes," the woman was shouting. "I must find those plasters at once. My poor feet!"

Rory and Elspeth looked at one another in a panic.

"They'll find us!" Rory whispered.

"Bathroom!" Elspeth replied.

They leaped in to the bathtub and drew the shower curtain across, just as the door to the cabin flew open.

"Frightful, frightful, frightful!" the woman was shouting.

Elspeth peeked around the curtain. She could just see the woman's bottom as she bent over, hauling everything out of a trunk and throwing it on the floor. "It's a DISASTER, Albert. I'm in agony. Take me home at once. I shan't sail."

"Oh, calm down, Petunia," said the man. "Come and have a nice drink up on deck."

"Nice drink!" Petunia whacked him over the head with a purse. "You stupid man — I can't walk another step in these shoes!"

"I believe Lord Spewitt might be up there," the man said in a sly voice.

"What? Why on earth didn't you say so?" shrilled his wife. "What are you standing about here for, you silly fool? Hurry, let's go!"

The door slammed shut again and Rory and Elspeth breathed out in relief.

"Right," Elspeth said. "We can't stay here. We need to get a better hiding place, so we can find Crabb and Goulash before they find us."

What Elspeth didn't know was that, at that very moment, Miss Crabb was directly beneath them, in the *HMS Unsinkable* Extremely Elegant Hair and Beauty Salon.

6

The Extremely Elegant
Hair and Beauty Salon

Poppy and Pippy, the ladies in charge of the
HMS Unsinkable Extremely Elegant Hair
and Beauty Salon, were setting down their
cases and looking around the smart new
salon in excitement. They were cousins who
came from a long line of ladies who had
done the hair of important people in history
– they had just finished a stint helping the

queen try out some new hairstyles.

"Isn't this ship smashing, Poppy?" said Pippy, who had long purple hair with a fringe.

"Yes, it's smashing, Pippy!" said Poppy, who wore her black hair in a sweeping style.

Poppy and Pippy were very cheerful ladies. They thought pretty much everything was smashing. But they *didn't* think it was smashing when a horrible smell filled the room and a claw-like hand appeared out of the large cupboard where their uniforms were kept.

"Aargh!" shrieked Poppy and Pippy, as Miss Crabb and Gladys Goulash lurched out of the cupboard.

Miss Crabb nabbed them as they tried to run out of the door. "Gotcha!" she cackled.

She grabbed a big pile of ribbons and tied them up tightly. Then she smirked.

"I'm sorry, my dears, but you are no longer needed on this ship," she said. "We will be taking over. YOU will be staying in that storeroom down the hall. Don't worry, we'll throw you some food and water every day! Eee-hee-hee!"

And with that, Miss Crabb and Gladys Goulash bundled Poppy and Pippy down the corridor and into a dark little room marked *Beauty Salon Store.*

They marched back into the salon looking smug. Then Miss Crabb threw a uniform at Gladys Goulash.

"Put this on," she ordered, wriggling into one herself. Miss Crabb was tall and skinny, so her uniform was too short. Gladys Goulash was short and wide, so her uniform was too tight. They looked in the mirror, putting their wigs back on and feeling very pleased with themselves. Miss Crabb's wig was just like Poppy's glamorous hair do and Gladys Goulash had a long purple wig with a fringe, like Pippy.

Gladys Goulash picked her nose and munched on a bogey thoughtfully.

"What do we have to do now?" she asked. "Are we hairdressers or something?"

"Gah!" said Miss Crabb. She sat down opposite Gladys and prodded her arm to make her pay attention. "We do hair *and* beauty. You know, painting toenails, that sort of thing. Remember, we have to pretend to be those ladies, Poppy and Pippy. We don't want to be found out."

Miss Crabb picked up a black crayon and drew a blob on her cheek. "Poppy has a beauty spot right here. And Pippy has big eyelashes." She took a pair of false eyelashes from her handbag and handed them to Gladys Goulash, who stuck them on and scratched her head.

"So remember," Miss Crabb said slowly, "your name is Pippy Delamere and you are a *trained beautician.*"

"And is this how we're going to make our millions?" asked Gladys.

"No, you fool!" cried Miss Crabb. She leaped up and started hopping from one foot to the other in frustration. "That's not the plan! The plan is to make it to New York where nobody knows us, so we can start making that Extra-special Sticky Toffee Sauce!"

"Ooh!" said Gladys. "I get it. Well, I'd better get practising." Gladys hauled herself to her feet and picked up a pair of scissors. "Shall I trim your hair for you?"

"This is not my hair, it's a wig, you nitwit!" shrieked Miss Crabb. "Practise painting your nails instead." She threw a bottle of nail varnish at Gladys. Then she stormed to the door, turning the sign around to say OPEN.

"Stay on your guard, Gladys Goulash," Miss Crabb said. "You're not a dinner lady any more. You are a beautician. And the *HMS Unsinkable* Extremely Elegant Hair and Beauty Salon is open for business. *Do not let me down.*"

Just then, the ship's whistle blew. It was almost time for the *HMS Unsinkable* to set sail.

7

The *HMS* Unsinkable Sets Sail

"We need a really good hiding place, somewhere safe," Elspeth said to Rory. "Once we have that, we can work out where the hair and beauty salon is. If anyone notices us, we'll say we're travelling with our parents." Elspeth felt sick with nerves. She'd never been on a boat before … let alone a cruise ship with two dangerous criminals on board.

Rory nodded. "You said we need to find Crabb and Goulash before they find us," he said. "Well, Lazlo can help with that. He'd sniff Gladys Goulash out if she was nearby."

"Good. Let's start exploring!" Elspeth said.

They opened the cabin door and peeked out. The coast was clear.

They climbed the stairs to the highest level on the ship and walked along a corridor so thickly carpeted that their feet sank into it. They passed a huge ballroom with a grand piano and sparkling chandeliers.

"That's even bigger than the ballroom in my house," Rory said in wonder. As they moved on, Lazlo started bopping up and down on his shoulder. "Lazlo can smell someone! We need to hide!" Rory said.

They ducked through a door into another corridor. This one was painted grey and it was much less fancy than the other parts of the ship they'd seen. They ran along it as fast as they could and, just as they turned a corner, they heard a slam followed by the sound of footsteps. Then they stopped short. They'd reached a dead end.

"What now?" Rory turned to Elspeth in fright. "We can't get out of here. We'll be caught!" He tucked Lazlo into his pocket to keep him out of sight.

"There's a ladder!" Elspeth rushed over to a red ladder attached to the wall and started climbing it. "We can go through this hatch."

They scrambled up and burst through the hatch, finding themselves on the main deck. Hundreds of people were milling about and drinking champagne. Rory quickly slammed the hatch closed behind them.

As they moved further into the crowd, the hatch burst open again. Elspeth and Rory froze.

A head appeared in the hatch, then a very cross face, then a large body in a tweed suit. It was Petunia, the lady whose cabin they'd hidden in. She staggered on to the deck, looking very upset.

"There you are, Albert!" she shrieked, throwing herself into her husband's arms. "You shouldn't have left me when I went to find the dining rooms. I took a wrong turn and ended up in the most GHASTLY corridor! It was painted the most depressing shade of grey. Oh, I feel quite seasick."

"You can't be seasick, dear, the ship isn't moving yet," said her husband, patting her on the back. "And there's a very calm forecast, so you've nothing to worry about."

Elspeth breathed out in relief. They weren't in any trouble … yet. Then she spotted a tall lady in a bright red dress, holding an angry-looking cat. "There's Lady Spewitt," she whispered to Rory. "She was mentioned in that newspaper article about the *HMS Unsinkable*. She and her husband are the richest couple in the UK. That's her cat, Tinkiewinks. He goes everywhere with her."

Rory looked worried. "Lazlo's really scared of cats," he said. "Let's move to the other side of the deck."

But before they could go anywhere, Tinkiewinks raised his nose in the air and

sniffed. He gave a hiss, leaped out of Lady
Spewitt's arms and shot towards Elspeth
and Rory. Lady Spewitt hurried after him
and Elspeth's heart started thumping as the
woman approached.

"Awfully excitable, aren't you,
Tinkiewinks?" Lady Spewitt said, scooping
up the cat and stroking his head.

She looked at Elspeth and Rory more
closely, glancing at Elspeth's rucksack and
her scruffy dress.

"Are you
two allowed
to be here by
yourselves?"
she asked
suspiciously.

"Oh yes, of course
we are!" Elspeth

replied, stepping in front of Rory. "Mummy and Daddy are just unpacking," she added.

Lady Spewitt raised her eyebrows then moved off, clutching Tinkiewinks tightly.

Rory gave a sigh of relief. "Lazlo's trembling, he's so terrified. We need to keep him away from that stupid cat or—"

His voice was drowned out by the sound of the ship's horn. A loud cheer went up from the passengers.

"We're off!" someone shouted.

And the *HMS Unsinkable*, with her 8,000 passengers and sparkling chandeliers and ballroom and swimming pool and fancy beauty salon, moved slowly away from the dock and started her very first voyage.

Elspeth and Rory leaned on the railing and gazed out at the crowds on the pier getting gradually smaller as the ship sailed away. But then Elspeth had an awful thought.

"Rory! What about Mum and Dad?" she gasped. "What if they come home, and I'm in New York? They'll *never* find me! What can I do?"

Rory thought fast. "It's OK," he said. "You can send a message in a bottle! Quick!" He grabbed an empty lemonade bottle from a nearby table and shook out the last drops. "Write them a note."

"Rory, that stuff only works in stories," Elspeth said in despair. "It won't get to them."

"Do it right now, before we're too far from shore," Rory said. "Come on, Elspeth. You're always telling me not to give up. It's worth a shot!"

Elspeth knew he was right. She scribbled

a quick note to her mum and dad and wrote their address on the other side of the paper. Then Rory shoved the message in the bottle, screwed the lid on tightly and handed it back to her. "Quickly," he said. "Don't let anyone see you."

Elspeth leaned out and threw the bottle over the side. The ship was so huge that they didn't even hear the splash when it landed in the water. Elspeth gazed down for a moment, then turned back to Rory.

"Come on," she said. "Let's go inside. We'll find a place to sleep tonight, then we can make a proper plan for getting the recipe back."

They slipped through the crowds and down some stairs. Elspeth paused in front of a door marked *Store*.

"This might be a good hiding place,"

she said. She opened the door and looked inside. It was empty, apart from a pile of blankets on a shelf and a broom in the corner. It was a small space, but it didn't look like it was used much. She flopped down on to the floor with a sigh.

"We can hide out here," she said. She got out her notebook. "I saw a sign saying the salon is down on level four of the ship – that's right at the bottom. I think I need to go on an exploring mission before we search for the recipe. That's what a detective would do – to get an idea of where everything is."

"That's a good start," Rory said. He got Lazlo out of his blazer pocket and let him have a run around. "I just hope no one comes in here."

Elspeth and Rory had no idea, dear

reader, that someone had been watching them creep along the passage. And that someone knew *exactly* where they were hiding.

8

The Not-so-secret Hiding Place

Just as Elspeth started sketching out a plan of the ship, she heard a noise. She glanced at Rory, who put his finger to his lips. They both stayed very still, staring at the door.

The handle started turning.

Elspeth jumped up as the door flew open.

A girl stood in the doorway. She was about the same age as them, with mousy blonde hair and bright blue eyes. And she looked angry.

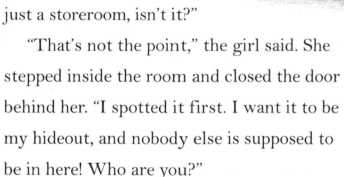

"What are you doing in my den?" the girl hissed.

Elspeth blinked in surprise. "Your den? It's just a storeroom, isn't it?"

"That's not the point," the girl said. She stepped inside the room and closed the door behind her. "I spotted it first. I want it to be my hideout, and nobody else is supposed to be in here! Who are you?"

"I'm Elspeth, and this is my friend, Rory," Elspeth said.

"And this is Lazlo," Rory said quickly.

Lazlo stared at the girl suspiciously.

The girl frowned. "Are your parents annoying you, too?" she asked, sounding a bit less cross. "That's why I wanted to hide out here. Mine are driving me mad. They make me go on a cruise with them every single summer – I think they're addicted! I feel like I've spent my life on cruise ships… I'm Cassie, by the way. Cassie Lovett. So, are you hiding out to get away from your mum and dad?"

Elspeth paused, thinking about what she could say. She glanced over at Rory, who gave a tiny shrug.

"Don't worry," said Cassie. "I'm just being friendly! Ooh, am I asking too many questions? Mum says I always do that…"

Elspeth chewed her lip. Cassie seemed nice, but how much should they tell her?

"It's just … our parents aren't on the boat," Elspeth said at last. "We sneaked on, and we'll be in so much trouble if we're caught. Please don't tell anyone you've seen us!"

"Wow," Cassie said. Her eyes grew even bigger. "You're … stowaways? That's so cool! But why are you heading to America? Are you running away from home?"

Again, Elspeth hesitated. She didn't want to give too much away.

Cassie stepped forward with a curious look on her face. "Are you in trouble?" she asked, sounding concerned. "You can tell me. I might be able to help you. I know my way around these ships. I can make sure you don't get caught."

Elspeth looked into Cassie's kind blue eyes and thought that she meant what

she said. Perhaps Cassie *could* help them …
but Elspeth would have to tell her the truth
first.

"It's a long story," Elspeth said. "Are you
sure you want to know? I don't want to get
you in trouble, too…"

Cassie nodded seriously. "Go on, you can
trust me. I promise."

"Well, I was kidnapped last year by two
criminals called Miss Crabb and Gladys
Goulash. They stole me from my mum and
dad –" Elspeth's eyes filled with tears, but
she was determined not to cry – "because I
had a top-secret recipe and they think it's
worth lots of money. They were keeping me
in a terrible boarding school—"

"Where Elspeth met me and Lazlo,"
interrupted Rory.

"And Rory helped me escape. But when

I got back home, Miss Crabb and Gladys Goulash came after me and stole the recipe from my house. They've sneaked on board this ship and now we're here because we *have* to get the recipe back."

"What? No way!" Cassie was silent for a second, shaking her head. "You're very brave. It all sounds awfully dangerous."

Elspeth raised her chin. "Maybe it is, but that recipe was very precious to my parents. I don't even know where my mum and dad are now – they went abroad looking for me. But I'm not letting those horrible women get away with stealing from us."

"Wow," Cassie said. "Well, it sounds like you've made up your mind. You can't stay here, though – someone might spot you. But I do know somewhere you could hide…"

Cassie led them along the corridor, down two flights of stairs and into a first-class section of the ship. She pushed open a door to reveal a magnificent cabin with two beds and a splendid view of the sea.

"Ta-daaa!" she said.

"We can't stay *here*," Elspeth said.

"No, honestly, you can!" Cassie grinned. "My mother travels with such a RIDICULOUS amount of luggage that they book an extra room when they sail, just in case. They don't need this space. They've forgotten it's even here!"

Cassie jumped up on one of the beds and bounced a few times.

Elspeth and Rory glanced at each other. Was it too good to be true?

"Why isn't *this* your den, if nobody comes in here?" Rory asked suspiciously.

"Because it's no fun staying somewhere I'm allowed to be," Cassie said. "It's much better to hide out in places where kids aren't supposed to go. Everyone keeps saying this boat is special, but it's got the exact same layout as a cruise ship we went on last year. I can show you around if you like. We could do it tonight! When the grown-ups are asleep."

"Will you take us to the hair and beauty salon?" asked Elspeth. "That's where Miss Crabb and Gladys Goulash will be. They're pretending to be hair and beauty ladies. But we'll have to be very careful, because I need to make sure they don't spot me! I just want to do a bit of exploring first of all, so I know what the salon is like."

Cassie nodded. "Definitely," she said. "I can show you the Extremely Elegant Hair and Beauty Salon tonight."

That night they sneaked around the ship after everyone else had gone to bed. They went into the kitchens and the dining room and the ballroom, and they even peeked in at the swimming pool, until Lazlo tried to go for a swim.

"I love swimming," Cassie said as Rory grabbed Lazlo from the edge of the pool. "Once I swam across the English Channel! And once I went on a cruise to the North Pole and swam with penguins!"

Elspeth wasn't sure she believed Cassie's wild stories, but their new friend was a very good guide. With Cassie's help, they crawled and climbed and jumped over all the interesting parts of the ship. Finally Cassie showed them the corridor leading to the hair and beauty salon.

"It's through there," she whispered, pointing.

Elspeth and Rory stared down the dark corridor. They were so close…

"Thanks, Cassie," Elspeth said softly. She took a deep breath. "I'm going to have to work out how to sneak in there. Once

I've seen the layout of the salon, then I can figure out how to find the recipe."

9

Miss Crabb and Gladys Goulash At Work

The *HMS Unsinkable* Extremely Elegant Hair and Beauty Salon looked fabulous. It had two rooms, big shiny mirrors with spotlights around them, lots of fluffy towels and comfortable chairs. And it *would* have been fabulous, if Poppy and Pippy were working there. But they were not. Poppy and Pippy were stuck in a storeroom feeling very sorry for themselves and eating a block of stale cheese for lunch. They kept banging on the door and shouting for help, but nobody could hear them.

In one room of the salon, Gladys Goulash was painting Lady Spewitt's toenails. Gladys had put on her favourite album, *Highland Bagpipe Classics*. I don't know if you have ever heard bagpipes, dear reader, but they really are quite difficult to listen to when they are played at top volume from a speaker that is right next to your head.

"Could you turn that music down a little?" asked Lady Spewitt impatiently.

"What? This music's my favourite!" said Gladys. Then she remembered she was supposed to be behaving herself. "I mean, yes, of course, I'm most terribly sorry, madam," she said in a fake-nice voice, turning the music off and giving Lady Spewitt her best smile.

In the next room, Miss Crabb was cutting the hair of the distinguished explorer, Baron Van Der Blink. She was doing her best, but his hair was rather uneven. Baron Van Der Blink looked worried, but Miss Crabb just grinned at him and kept on cutting.

"Lovely hair you've got," she said. "This style is what everyone is asking for in, um, Iceland."

"Iceland?" Baron Van Der Blink said in confusion. "I've visited Iceland. I didn't see anyone with hair like this."

"Ooh, yes, that's where I was trained – they've got lovely haircuts in Iceland," said Miss Crabb, making it up as she went along. "In fact, I won an award for Iceland's Hairchopper of the Century!"

"Of the *century*?" Baron Van Der Blink said suspiciously. He wriggled around in his chair a bit. "You're the best hairdresser they've had in a *hundred years*?"

Miss Crabb didn't like all these questions. She threw the scissors down. "There you are. Done! Isn't it lovely?"

Baron Van Der Blink looked at his

reflection doubtfully. "I'm not sure it's all the same length," he said.

"Course it is!" Miss Crabb said firmly. "You look ever so handsome." She helped him up and gave him a big grin. "That will be fifty pounds, please."

Baron Van Der Blink shrugged, then took out his wallet and handed over the money. He walked away slowly, touching the back of his head.

When he'd left, Miss Crabb slammed the door and stuffed the fifty-pound note down her jumper. "Nice bit of extra cash," she muttered. "That'll buy me some lovely new false teeth when we get to New York."

Just then the door flew open and Gladys Goulash plodded in, followed by Lady Spewitt, who was looking slightly cross.

Miss Crabb gave what she thought was

a friendly smile, but she looked like a dog baring its teeth. "Thank you for visiting the Extremely Elegant Hair and Beauty Salon! I hope you've enjoyed your experience."

Lady Spewitt scowled. "Well, I suppose it was fine – once she'd turned off that awful music!"

Miss Crabb flared her nostrils and gave Gladys Goulash her sternest glare.

Then she clasped her hands together and smiled at Lady Spewitt.

"I'm so terribly sorry," Miss Crabb said in a sugary voice. "There'll be no charge – and I do hope you'll come back another day."

Lady Spewitt nodded and left, looking rather dazed.

As soon as the door had closed behind her, Miss Crabb threw a pot of hair gel at Gladys Goulash's head.

"You nincompoop!" Miss Crabb hollered. "You've upset the customer! You have to keep them happy or they'll realize we're fakes!"

The ship gave a sudden lurch and sent Miss Crabb flying into a pile of dirty towels.

"You need to do better, Gladys Goulash," she cried, struggling to get up. "Or I'll throw you to the sharks!"

10
The Ship
Begins to Lurch

Elspeth woke up the next morning with a
jolt when Rory's alarm clock went off. For
a second she couldn't think where on earth
she was, then in a flash she remembered she
was on the *HMS Unsinkable*, and Cassie had
sneaked them into a fancy cabin.

Elspeth got up with a strange feeling
in the pit of her stomach. The ship

was swaying from side to side, and it was making her feel funny. Then she remembered that she was going to do some detective work in the Extremely Elegant Hair and Beauty Salon, and that made her stomach churn even more.

I have to be brave, Elspeth thought to herself as she got washed and dressed. *It's worth the risk if I can get Mum and Dad's recipe back.*

She heard Cassie's special knock: three knocks, then two, then one. That was how they knew it was safe to open the cabin door.

"Ready?" Cassie grinned at them. "Exploring mission: GO!"

They all hurried down to the lowest level of the ship, holding on to the railings to keep themselves steady as the ship tipped from side to side.

"Urgh, I'm not sure I like being at sea," Rory said, as they arrived at the corridor leading to the salon. He looked a bit green. "Be very careful, Elspeth," he added. "Don't let them see you."

"I will be careful," said Elspeth, "but I need to do this. Otherwise I've got no way of knowing where things are in the salon, and where Crabb and Goulash sleep. You two keep lookout. If I'm not back in five minutes, I need help!"

"Good luck!" they whispered.

As she walked down the corridor, Elspeth thought for a second that she could hear a muffled banging, but when she paused to listen, it had stopped. She took a deep breath and kept going until she reached a glass door with the words *Extremely Elegant Hair and Beauty Salon* on it. Very carefully, Elspeth leaned forward until she could see inside.

Even under that terrible wig, she could clearly see that the woman scribbling in a greasy old notebook was Miss Crabb. Gladys Goulash was with her, slowly counting a pile of fifty-pound notes and burping. Elspeth gave a shiver at seeing them so close.

She peered in, trying to guess where they might have hidden the recipe. In one of the cupboards, maybe? Or in the box with the fifty-pound notes? But Elspeth couldn't get any nearer without being seen. She looked further down the corridor and noticed an open door, revealing a very untidy cabin. An awful smell was coming from inside, and Elspeth could just make out two beds and a pile of clothes on the floor. But she didn't dare go closer in case Crabb and Goulash spotted her through the glass door.

She moved quietly back along the corridor to Cassie and Rory, who were hiding behind a big display of fancy flowers.

"I saw their cabin!" she told them. "I'll need to search in there as well as in the salon. But how can we get both of them out of the way for long enough?" she said. "Cassie, what happens on a ship like this if someone sets off a fire alarm?"

"Oh, everyone's supposed to get up on deck, where there are meeting stations that you wait at," Cassie said.

"Hmm," Elspeth said. "I wonder…"

Elspeth Hart had a very interesting idea.

11
The *HMS Unsinkable* Fire Alarm

The next morning, Elspeth waited next to the fire alarm on the third level. She felt very nervous. Smashing a fire alarm was pretty high up on the list of Naughty Things You Must Not Ever Do, but then again, so was stowing away on a cruise ship. And so were kidnapping people and stealing top-secret recipes. Elspeth took a deep breath and bashed the fire alarm with her elbow.

The siren was so loud that Elspeth had to cover her ears with her hands while she ran away as fast as she could. She raced down the nearest staircase and paused in an alcove, pressing her back hard against the wall, but nobody noticed her. Everyone was too busy panicking.

Jimmy McScoff the chef abandoned the huge pan of soup he was stirring and gave a yelp of fright before rushing his staff up to their emergency meeting point.

Petunia Galoshes-Gallop fainted and had to be carried up on deck by her husband.

Lady Spewitt grabbed Tinkiewinks and piled on all her diamond necklaces at once. "I shan't leave my jewels here – if we escape in a lifeboat, they're coming with me," she announced.

And down in the Extremely Elegant Hair and Beauty Salon, Miss Crabb screeched, "Fire! I'm off! Save yourselves!" and shot out of the door and up the stairs two at a time. Gladys Goulash followed her and the customers ran after them with shampoo suds in their hair.

Elspeth Hart waited until the sound of hurried footsteps died down. Then, when she was absolutely sure there was no one around, she made her way into the Extremely Elegant Hair and Beauty Salon. She rifled through make-up and bottles of shampoo and the box of fifty-pound notes. She looked under tables and in cupboards and drawers and in every nook and cranny she could find, but after searching the whole place, there was no sign of the precious recipe.

It could be in their cabin, Elspeth thought. *Or maybe Miss Crabb keeps the recipe with her...* But just as she started moving across the corridor towards the cabin, a loud voice came over the tannoy.

"LADIES AND GENTLEMEN, THIS WAS A FALSE ALARM, THERE IS

NO FIRE! PLEASE FEEL FREE TO RETURN TO YOUR CABINS."

Elspeth was running out of time. She tried the handle of the cabin door, but it was locked. She started hurrying back down the corridor, but then she heard thudding footsteps and a shrill voice she recognized.

"Get back in that salon right now, Gladys Goulash! We've got to finish washing the customers' hair!"

As you know, dear reader, Elspeth was brave and determined and quick-thinking, but the sound of Miss Crabb and Gladys Goulash coming closer threw her into a panic. She gave a squeak of fear as she looked around for a place to hide. Where could she go? The cabin was locked, the corridor behind her was a dead end, and any minute now Miss Crabb would march through the doors and catch her. There was only one thing for it. Elspeth rushed back into the salon and dived beneath a pile of towels, pulling them over her head. She stayed perfectly still, even as the ship rolled gently from side to side, and prayed she wouldn't be spotted.

"Gah! Where are those customers? They haven't paid us yet!" Miss Crabb was stomping around in a rage. "Go and find them, Gladys Goulash. Go on!"

Elspeth heard the door slam. She peeped through a little gap in the pile of towels. What on earth could she do now?

"Stupid customers," Miss Crabb muttered grumpily. She threw herself down in one of the hairdressing chairs.

After a few minutes, Miss Crabb gave a great yawn.

"Might as well have a little snooze," Elspeth heard her say.

Elspeth remembered that at the Pandora Pants School for Show-offs, Miss Crabb liked to have a nap whenever she could. She watched closely as Miss Crabb leaned back in the chair and shut her eyes.

Please, please fall into a deep sleep so I can get out of here, thought Elspeth.

She waited in the pile of towels, not daring to move a muscle. She was in luck — in under a minute, Miss Crabb was snoring loudly with her mouth wide open. Elspeth slipped out from under the towels and crept quietly towards the door. But as she turned the handle, she glanced over to see Miss Crabb sitting up.

Her eyes were open.

She was staring straight at Elspeth.

12
Miss Crabb's Staring Eyes

It is quite amazing, dear reader, that Elspeth Hart did not scream at the top of her voice. She gave a yelp, but slapped her hand over her mouth to stop the sound.

Miss Crabb didn't blink.

Elspeth wanted to run, but she couldn't. It was as if she was stuck to the floor, she was so terrified.

Then Miss Crabb gave a huge snort and sank back down. Her eyes closed and she started snoring again.

Elspeth stared at her for a few more seconds, unable to move. Miss Crabb was still asleep! She must have sat up and opened her eyes *in her sleep*!

She had escaped Miss Crabb's clutches this time … but only just.

"I think you're ever so brave," Cassie said
that evening, handing Elspeth and Rory
some sausage rolls she'd sneaked from the
dinner table. "You knew those horrible
ladies could have caught you. It was so
dangerous. Almost as dangerous as the time
I jumped off a ship and swam with sharks,
and then climbed back up without anyone
noticing!"

Elspeth and Rory looked at each other.
Cassie's stories were getting more and more
unbelievable.

"It was scary," Elspeth said. "But I'm
not giving up. That recipe could be in their
cabin. I need to get in there to search it!"

She put down her napkin and sausage roll.
She felt too nervous to eat, so she lay back on

her bed. The great ship had started to roll even more on the choppy seas.

"Apparently we're in for some stormy weather," said Cassie. "The grown-ups were all talking about it at dinner. I hope neither of you get seasick! I never do. I'm totally not scared *at all*."

Elspeth wasn't paying attention. She was staring upwards and she'd noticed something strange. The ceiling wasn't smooth, like in a normal room. It was made up of lots of large panels.

Elspeth sat up very suddenly. "There are panels in the ceiling of every cabin," she said. "I wonder…"

She jumped up on her bed and pushed at one of the panels with her hands. Sure enough, the panel popped up and a cold draft blew in.

"Wow! What's up there?" asked Rory. Lazlo scampered up to take a look.

"Oh, nothing much – just pipes and stuff," said Cassie. "You can crawl along above all the rooms – they use it for maintenance. A boy on a cruise last summer went up for a dare, but he got really scared and came straight back down again!" Cassie laughed, but then she saw Elspeth's face.

She was staring up into the dark space with a thoughtful look in her eyes.

"Wait, you're not going up there, are you?" Cassie asked. "I wouldn't. I mean, I'm not scared or anything, but it's really dark."

"Yes!" Elspeth said. "This is how I can get into Crabb and Goulash's cabin! It's perfect!"

Rory was shaking his head. "Elspeth, I'm not sure about this…"

"Don't worry!" Elspeth said. "If the crawl space is totally secret, like Cassie says, then Crabb and Goulash will never know I'm there. I'll just wait until they're both busy in the salon, then I'll sneak into their cabin."

"Blimey, you're really going to do it." Cassie swallowed. She went quiet, but not for long. "Well, I heard my mum saying she's getting her hair done tomorrow at four, so we know for certain that they'll be busy in the salon then. Do you think you could sneak in, Elspeth? It seems awfully risky…"

"It *is* risky," Elspeth said. She stared up into the musty space above her head. "But that's exactly what I have to do."

13
Four O'Clock the Next Afternoon

Elspeth had to fight to stay calm as she slithered along in the crawl space above the rooms down on level four. Cassie had said it would be pitch dark, but it wasn't just that — it was also very narrow and the dust kept making her cough. And to make matters worse, the ship was rolling from side to side, even more violently than before.

Elspeth was glad Rory and Lazlo were right behind her.

"Just five more panels," she whispered. She had worked out exactly how far they would have to go to reach the cabin. She crawled along in the darkness, counting down the panels, then pulled up the one ahead of her and peered inside the room.

The horrible mess and the disgusting smell told her at once that it was Miss Crabb and Gladys Goulash's cabin.

"Bingo," Elspeth said. "We're in the right spot." She glanced behind her and saw Rory's pale face in the darkness.

"Good luck," he hissed. "Be quick. When you're ready to come back up, I'll reach down and help you. I'm keeping an eye on the time."

Elspeth drew her head back inside the shaft and wriggled until her feet were sticking down into the room. Then she let herself drop lower and lower until she landed with a soft thud on one of the beds.

She jumped up at once and looked around. Miss Crabb's spare false teeth were sitting in a glass by the side of the bed. The smell was even stronger now Elspeth was inside the room. It smelled like a mixture of old cabbage and dirty socks.

"Yuck," Elspeth said. But she didn't have

time to worry about the smell. She searched high and low for the precious recipe. She went through Miss Crabb's horrible shiny blouses with sweat patches, and through Gladys Goulash's dresses with stains and smears all over them. She searched and searched until she was about to give up. But just as she heard Rory hiss at her to come back up, Elspeth Hart lifted up Miss Crabb's pillow and found…

Elspeth picked up the diary and flicked to the most recent entry. She had to cling on to the bedside table to stay upright as the ship swayed from side to side.

"Pssst! Elspeth! Time to get out of there!" came Rory's anxious voice.

Elspeth glanced up. "Thirty more seconds!" she said. "I've got Crabb's secret diary here!"

She scanned the page.

Friday 13th July

Eee-hee-hee! I've already made hundreds of pounds - I can use the money to set up our Extra-special Sticky Toffee Sauce factory as soon as we get to America. Stupid Gladys can do all the work and I'll be the boss. I'll have a lovely time snoozing in the sun while she makes the sauce! I'm keeping the recipe where nobody would dare to look, because there are too many spying eyes.

Eee-hee-hee!

Elspeth was dying to read on, but she could hear footsteps outside.

"Hurry!" Rory was reaching his hands out towards Elspeth. "They're coming!"

Elspeth stuffed the diary back under the pillow and jumped up on to the bed. She grabbed Rory's hands and he pulled her upwards until she could scramble the rest of the way herself. They slammed the panel closed and sat on it, breathing heavily and not daring to make a noise. Even Lazlo was still for once.

The key turned in the lock and they heard Miss Crabb come into the room. She muttered and stomped about for a bit, then Gladys plodded in. Elspeth pressed her ear against the panel and strained to hear.

"They've been banging and shouting again, them two in the storeroom," Gladys complained. "Can't we shut them up?"

"Gah! Stupid little rat-faces," Miss Crabb said. "They probably want food. Fling them some of those tomatoes from lunch."

"I've done that," Gladys said. "They went quiet for a bit, but then they started up again."

"I'll deal with them, Gladys Goulash," said Miss Crabb. The icy calm of her voice made her sound very sinister indeed.

Elspeth could see Rory's eyes get bigger as they listened. *What is Crabb up to now?* she wondered. She pointed back along the tunnel, and she and Rory slithered to safety.

"You found her *diary*? No way!" Cassie said.

They were in their cabin, telling Cassie what had happened, and brushing off the dust and cobwebs.

"Did it tell you anything useful?" asked Cassie.

"It said that the recipe was hidden somewhere nobody would dare to look!" Elspeth said.

Rory shuddered. "That could be *anywhere* in their room."

"No, wait, it also said something about eyes." Elspeth was wiping the dirt from her hands. She paused, screwed up her nose and tried to remember. "*Nobody would dare to look, because there are too many spying eyes.*"

"What on earth does that mean?" Cassie said.

"I'm not sure. I haven't worked it out yet," Elspeth said. "But there's more. Rory, did you hear Gladys Goulash saying two people were 'banging and shouting'?

And Miss Crabb said she'd take care of it. It sounded like they had prisoners. You know who that must be…"

"Poppy and Pippy!" said Rory. "The real hair and beauty ladies!"

Elspeth nodded. "Crabb and Gladys Goulash haven't just taken their place – they've got them locked up on board the ship! And we're the only people who know they've been taken prisoner," she said. "We *have* to get them out."

14
Miss Crabb's Troublesome Prisoners

As you know, dear reader, Miss Crabb and
Gladys Goulash had no idea that Elspeth
Hart was on board the ship. Which is just as
well, as they already had plenty of problems
to deal with. Miss Crabb hadn't bargained
on Poppy and Pippy being quite so much
trouble. They hadn't given up banging and
shouting, and it was becoming rather hard

to cover up the noise. In fact, they seemed to get louder every day.

When Jimmy McScoff the chef came in for a haircut on the fourth day of the voyage, he was sure he could hear a strange thumping noise. To make things worse, the sea had become horribly choppy, so Miss Crabb was struggling to stay steady on her feet. She got halfway through Jimmy McScoff's haircut, then gave up using scissors and spiked it all up with a comb.

He looked at himself in the mirror uncertainly. "I'm not sure this is quite what I asked for..." he said. Then the thumping noise came from down the corridor, louder this time. "What's that?" he asked, trying to get up and have a look.

Miss Crabb pushed him firmly back into the chair. "Not finished yet!" she shrieked.

"We need to put some more hairspray on that lovely top section." She hurried into the next room, where Gladys Goulash was supposed to be cleaning. Instead she was dipping her finger into a pot of hair dye and tasting it. This, dear reader, is a dangerous and deadly thing to do, and you should never try it at home. Ever.

"Get in that room and make some noise," Miss Crabb hissed, dragging Gladys away from the hair dye. "The chef can hear banging from down the corridor. You need to distract him. Put on your music and do some dancing."

"Dancing? I can't do dancing!" said Gladys. "You know how I feel about exercise. I haven't done any for years."

"Do it, turnip brain!" Miss Crabb grabbed Gladys Goulash's arm and hauled her back into the other room. She grinned at Jimmy McScoff, showing her yellow teeth. "My colleague will now perform a traditional dance for you," said Miss Crabb.

"Look, I haven't got time for this," said Jimmy McScoff. He tried to stand up again, but Miss Crabb pushed him back down. "She'd be so insulted if you left," she said smoothly, patting him on the arm. "It's only polite to stay."

Miss Crabb jabbed at the CD player and Gladys's *Highland Bagpipe Classics* started playing at top volume.

Dear reader, you may have seen amazing things, either in real life or on TV. Maybe you have seen monsters. Maybe you have seen elephants or sloths. But you have never seen anything like Gladys Goulash dancing on a cruise ship in the middle of a storm.

First she stamped one foot, then the next.
Then she whirled her arms around so a
strong smell of sweat wafted over to Jimmy
McScoff. She jumped up and down, which
made the whole room shudder, and then she
tried to do a spin and fell on her bum.

The thudding and squealing of the bagpipes meant that Jimmy McScoff completely forgot about the strange thumping noise.

Miss Crabb narrowed her eyes. She would have to shut up Poppy and Pippy for good … before they gave her away.

Back in their cabin, Elspeth, Cassie and Rory were sitting on the floor in a circle. Huge waves crashed against the porthole, and every so often Rory looked outside and gave a shudder. The storm was making the ship lurch from side to side.

"So," Elspeth said, "this is the plan. I'll go back through the ventilation shaft into Crabb's cabin tomorrow, when we know they're busy in the beauty salon. Rory, you come with me like last time, to help me get back out again. I'm going to find that recipe if it's the last thing I do!"

"What about me? What can I do?" asked Cassie.

"Well, we've got to rescue Poppy and Pippy, too," Elspeth said. She thought for a moment. "When Miss Crabb realizes the recipe is missing, she'll probably start charging around looking for it," Elspeth said. "At that point, you could sneak into Crabb and Goulash's cabin, grab her keys and release Poppy and Pippy from the salon storeroom!"

"Yes!" Cassie said, her eyes bright.

"Great," said Elspeth. She pulled the newspaper out of her rucksack and handed it to Cassie. "Once you've done that, you'll have to go straight to the captain. Show her the newspaper as proof and tell her what Miss Crabb and Gladys Goulash are up to."

Cassie tucked the paper under her arm. "I can do that," she said, sounding excited. "But what will you do, once you've got the recipe back?"

"As soon as we get the recipe, we'll come back here to our cabin and stay out of sight," Elspeth said. "Then, when the ship docks in New York, we'll need to sneak off without being seen."

"But why?" Cassie looked confused. "Once everyone knows that Miss Crabb and Gladys Goulash are criminals, they'll look after you, won't they?"

"The thing is, I don't want to be looked after!" Elspeth explained. "Once I've got the recipe back, I need to find my parents. I don't trust grown-ups to help me. If they get involved, they'll put me in some horrible place for children, which would probably be even worse than the Pandora Pants School for Show-offs. Then they'd take over the searching and not let me do anything. I can't let that happen!"

As she spoke, Elspeth realized that Rory was looking very serious. "Rory, are you OK?" she asked.

Rory gulped and nodded. "Just a bit seasick. It's a dangerous plan, Elspeth," he said, "but I trust you. Count me in."

15
Elspeth's Dangerous Plan

The next day, the *HMS Unsinkable* pitched and lurched on a dark and stormy sea, as Elspeth and Rory made their way along the ventilation shaft above Miss Crabb and Gladys Goulash's cabin. Elspeth's heart was banging so loudly that she was worried it would give them away. She tried not to think about what Miss Crabb would do if she caught her. Take her prisoner? Lock her in a cupboard? Or something truly terrible, like throwing her into a sea full of hungry sharks? Elspeth took a deep breath to calm herself. She thought about Miss Crabb getting away with her parents' secret recipe and narrowed her eyes. She *couldn't* let that happen.

Elspeth raised the panel gently and peered down. The cabin was empty. Just like before, there were plates of half-eaten food lying around and lots of dirty clothes. This time the heating was on full blast, too, and the cabin was horribly hot and stuffy.

Elspeth dropped into the room and paused at the foot of one of the beds. She thought back to Miss Crabb's secret diary. *'Where nobody would dare to look … too many spying eyes…'*

Where haven't I looked? Elspeth asked herself. She quickly opened up Miss Crabb's suitcase, but it was empty. She peered under the bed, but could only see banana skins and dirty socks. And then she spotted something that she recognized – Miss Crabb's sweetie jar. It used to sit in a dark, sticky corner of the pantry in the Pandora Pants School for Show-offs. Miss Crabb loved to eat big gobstoppers, and she used to scare the smaller children by threatening to steal their eyes and turn them into sweets.

"Spying eyes!" Elspeth murmured to herself. "Could it be…?"

She reached under the bed and pulled out the glass jar. The eyeball gobstoppers stared up at her as Elspeth turned the jar upside down and shook it hard.

Sure enough, there was a piece of paper wedged in there, folded up very small. Elspeth took the lid off the jar and poured the gobstoppers out on to the bed. She pulled the paper out and opened it up, hardly daring to look. But she recognized her own handwriting at once.

Hart's Extra-special Sticky Toffee Sauce

Sugar: 55g

Butter: 55g

Syrup: 1 tablespoon

Vanilla: 1/2 teaspoon

Treacle: 1 teaspoon

Cream: 200 ml

She finally had the recipe back.

Just at that moment, the storm quietened down. The ship stopped rocking from side to side and Elspeth stood still for a second, clutching the recipe tightly in her hand. It was the most wonderful feeling.

But then the spell was broken by the sound of heavy footsteps coming down the corridor.

"Elspeth! Hurry!" Rory hissed.

Elspeth shoved the recipe into her trainer, pushing it down as far as it would go, and hurled herself up on to the bed. She jumped up and grabbed Rory's hands. He pulled as hard as he could, and Elspeth kicked and squirmed to get her legs inside the hatch.

"Quickly!" Rory cried.

But Elspeth wasn't quick enough.

Her feet were
still dangling down
when the door flew
open. And Miss
Crabb spotted her at
once.

16
Miss Crabb's
Claw-like Hands

"You little varmint, what are you doing here?" shrilled Miss Crabb at the top of her lungs. She launched herself across the room and grabbed Elspeth's ankle.

Elspeth struggled, clinging on to Rory, but it was no use – Miss Crabb was stronger. She hauled at Elspeth's foot with her claw-like hands until Elspeth couldn't hang on any more, and she tumbled down on to the bed.

Rory's terrified face peeked out of the hatch and Miss Crabb reached up and grabbed him, too, dragging him out by his jacket and chucking him on to the bed with a bump.

"You little snotrags," sneered Miss Crabb. She spotted the gobstopper jar lying on the bed. "Thought you could steal back that recipe? No chance. What have you done with it?"

It's not your recipe, it's mine, Elspeth thought angrily. She pretended to look down sadly, but as she lowered her head, she sneakily glanced left and right. Was there anything she could use to escape? There was a huge pile of disgusting pants lying on the bed next to her.

"Right, I shall just have to search your pockets myself!" Miss Crabb shrieked.

But as Miss Crabb reached out to grab her, Elspeth ducked to the side, picked up the biggest pair of pants she could see, and flung them over her enemy's head. Then she shoved Miss Crabb as hard as she could.

"Aaaarf!" shouted Miss Crabb, toppling over and struggling to get the pants off her head.

"RUN!" Elspeth shouted to Rory.

They raced out of the cabin and along the corridor. Elspeth could hear Miss Crabb's voice behind them.

"Follow me, Gladys Goulash!" she was shrieking. "Help me catch those little brats!"

Elspeth didn't dare look over her shoulder. She ran as fast as she could.

Elspeth knew Miss Crabb would stop at nothing to get the recipe. She and Rory launched themselves up three flights of stairs and into the kitchens with Miss Crabb behind them. She was so close that they could hear her wheezy breath.

"What the heck do you kids think you're doing?" hollered Jimmy McScoff, as Elspeth and Rory raced through, knocking over a big vat of orange jelly.

"What's the plan, Elspeth?" gasped Rory.

"Just keep running!" Elspeth said.

Miss Crabb wasn't far behind. She ran into the kitchen, skidded through the orange jelly and landed right in a huge chocolate cake.

"I just iced that cake, you idiot woman!" cried Jimmy McScoff.

"Gah!" Miss Crabb shouted. She clambered to her feet, shoved Jimmy McScoff out of the way, leaving a big chocolatey handprint on his chest, and hobbled on.

Ahead of her, Elspeth and Rory burst into the empty dining room, swerving round chairs and tables, and skidding on the polished floor, as they weaved their way to the other side and out into a wide corridor.

They hurtled up another flight of stairs and ran towards the ballroom. They couldn't hear Miss Crabb any more, but they knew she couldn't be far behind.

"Faster!" cried Elspeth.

Then Rory gave a shout. "Lazlo! No!"

There was a loud miaow from further down the corridor, and they could hear Lady Spewitt speaking to Tinkiewinks.

Lazlo leaped from Rory's shoulder and shot across the corridor into the ballroom.

"Lazlo! Come back!" cried Rory and, before Elspeth could stop him, he raced into the ballroom after Lazlo.

"No!" Elspeth hissed. "We have to keep going!"

But it was too late. Rory was gone.

17
The Dangerous Daily Tea Dance

Elspeth stared through the window in the double doors, her heart racing. The ballroom was full of elegant people twirling and swaying at the daily tea dance. Most of the passengers fancied themselves as rather good dancers, and the dance always went ahead, no matter how choppy the sea was. Even if you think you are an excellent dancer, dear reader, you would find it quite a challenge to dance on a floor that keeps tilting from side to side. But since the storm had calmed down, the ballroom was full.

Rory raced after Lazlo, right on to the dance floor. Before he knew it, he was swept around in a circle by Petunia Galoshes-Gallop, who was wearing an enormous peach ballgown. She screwed up her eyes as she looked down at Rory.

"I say. I don't have my glasses on, so I'm afraid I don't recognize you," she said. "You're a bit of a blur. Are you one of Lord Spewitt's friends?" She twirled Rory around again at top speed before he could answer. "You're rather short, aren't you?"

Petunia Galoshes-Gallop was spinning Rory so fast that his feet were hardly touching the ground.

Elspeth couldn't wait a second longer – she could hear Miss Crabb coming up the stairs. She ran in after Rory, swerving through the couples on the dance floor. There was a long table at the far side of the ballroom and Elspeth flung herself under it, hiding behind the tablecloth before anyone noticed her.

She peeked out from under the tablecloth and spotted Lazlo instantly. She reached out and grabbed him. He bit her twice before she managed to wrestle a piece of chocolate from her pocket and offer it to him, which seemed to calm him down. Then Elspeth froze. A pair of feet in huge orange high-heeled shoes had appeared next to the table. Elspeth recognized the shoes: they belonged to Lady Spewitt.

Elspeth could feel Lazlo trembling
with fear ... which meant only one thing –
Tinkiewinks. The orange high heels were
so close that Elspeth could have reached
out and touched them.

Elspeth knew she had to make a run for
it before Lazlo escaped, but what if Miss
Crabb had followed them into the ballroom?

She shuffled her way back to the other side of the table and peeked out. She couldn't see Miss Crabb anywhere. The double doors to the corridor were at the far side of the dance floor. She could see Rory near them, still being whirled around by Petunia Galoshes-Gallop.

Here goes, thought Elspeth. She clung on to Lazlo and darted out from under the table, snatching Rory's hand as she passed him and shoving him in front of her through the double doors. They went flying off down the corridor before anyone could get a proper look at them.

"Thanks, Elspeth!" Rory puffed as they raced along the corridor. "It looks like we've lost Crabb for now—"

BOOF! Before he could finish his sentence, Elspeth and Rory turned a corner and banged into something. Something knobbly and pointy and tall.

Elspeth looked up in horror.

It was Miss Crabb.

18

The Knobbly Shape
of Miss Crabb

Miss Crabb grabbed Elspeth and Rory by
their shoulders, digging her fingers in so
hard it made them wince.

"Gotcha," she said softly.

Gladys Goulash plodded up and plonked
herself behind them so Elspeth and Rory
were stuck between their enemies. There
was no way out.

Miss Crabb dragged them up some stairs and on to the empty windswept deck. Gladys Goulash clutched Elspeth and Rory by the hair to stop them from running away and Miss Crabb stood before them, her arms folded.

Elspeth could feel Rory quivering with fear next to her. The wind whistled around them and rain started to fall.

"Nice try, Elspeth," said Miss Crabb. "But you're not smart enough to outwit me. Hand over that recipe now, or I'll dangle you over the side of the ship until you do."

Elspeth's mind raced. Would anyone come to their rescue? She had to give Cassie time to release Poppy and Pippy and tell the captain what was going on. If she could stall Miss Crabb for long enough, perhaps they would be saved…

"Before we talk about the recipe," Elspeth said, trying to sound calm, "tell me where my parents are. You know, don't you! You lured them away with a phone call saying I was abroad."

"I don't know where your parents are," sneered Miss Crabb.

"Yes, you do," interrupted Gladys Goulash.

"You told them to look for Elspeth in Australi—"

"Shut it, you gibbering goat!" Miss Crabb hissed. She gave Gladys Goulash her most evil stare, and Gladys was silent.

Australia! Elspeth thought.

"And I know you broke into my house and stole the recipe," Elspeth added.

"So what?" Miss Crabb said. "You won't be telling anyone about any of this, you stupid child. I'm going to get that recipe back, and get rid of you and your pesky friend once and for all." She started moving closer, with an evil glint in her eye.

"Keep a lookout, Gladys Goulash," she ordered, and then she pounced.

Elspeth squealed, but before she had time to squirm away, Miss Crabb had flipped her upside down.

Suddenly Elspeth Hart was dangling over the side of the *HMS Unsinkable*, staring in terror at the sea below.

19

Peril on the
HMS Unsinkable

While Miss Crabb was dangling Elspeth over the side of the ship, Cassie burst into the ballroom. She'd released Poppy and Pippy, and they were now trailing after her, looking very confused. She marched straight to the front of the room and tapped the captain on the shoulder.

"I have something very important to

tell you," Cassie said to the captain.

Captain Steel smiled kindly at Cassie. "I'm afraid I'm about to dance with Baron Van Der Blink, young lady," she said. "Can it wait?"

The Baron gave a bow and held out his hand.

"No, you've got to listen, it's important!" Cassie said, following them on to the dance floor and trying to grab the captain's arm.

"Buzz off, you little pest," said Baron Van Der Blink, looking down at her impatiently.

They twirled away into the crowd. Cassie looked around and decided there was only one thing for it. She shoved her way to where the band were playing and climbed up on to a chair, but the grown-ups still weren't paying attention to her.

"LADIES AND GENTLEMEN, YOUR ATTENTION PLEASE!" she shouted at the top of her voice.

Everyone turned to stare at her. The band stopped playing, the grown-ups stopped what they were doing, and the room fell totally silent.

Cassie's mother broke the spell. "Cassie Lovett," she shouted. "You get down from there right now."

"No, Mother, I shan't," Cassie said. "You need to hear this. Everyone does. These poor ladies –" she pointed at Poppy and Pippy, who were waiting nervously at the edge of the dance floor – "have had a terrible ordeal. They are the hair and beauty ladies who were supposed to be working on this ship. But two criminals locked them in a storeroom! The hair and beauty ladies that you've all seen – they're fakes!"

A gasp of shock rippled around the room.

"Look!" Cassie unrolled the newspaper and held it up. "The ladies you see here today were the ones booked to work on this ship. Here's their picture in the newspaper.

But the two women who locked them up
are called Miss Crabb and Gladys Goulash,
and they escaped from jail just a few days
ago." She flipped to the front page and held
it high for everyone to see. "Miss Crabb and
Gladys Goulash are dangerous criminals,
and you've GOT to stop them!"

Petunia Galoshes-Gallop leaped up
in fright, knocking over a whole platter
of sandwiches, and started pulling at her
husband's hand.

"Criminals on board!" she cried. "To the
lifeboats! We must escape!"

This sent the rest of the passengers
into a terrible panic. If you can imagine
a stampede of wild animals, dear reader,
then you can imagine the sight of the
passengers on the *HMS Unsinkable* in
hysterics.

Petunia shoved her way through the crowds, grabbing a stack of pancakes from the tea-trolley. Her husband hurried after her, hitting anyone in his way with a half-eaten kipper.

Lady Spewitt burst into tears and accidentally whacked her husband in the face with her handbag.

One couple tried to smash a porthole to get out, and several more started arming themselves with spoons and butter knives.

Some passengers began flinging fruit at one another and in under a minute the ballroom looked like the world's poshest, messiest food fight.

Custard was dripping from the chandeliers. People were chucking around cream cakes like snowballs. It was the most dreadful mess.

"Please will you calm down and return to your seats!" the captain cried, but everyone ignored her.

Finally she yelled at the top of her voice, "YOU LOT SIT DOWN AND SHUT UP NOW!"

It worked. The wealthy passengers weren't used to being told what to do. They all sat down at once and went very quiet.

Captain Steel looked around the room. She had been a captain for many years and there wasn't much that scared her. She had come across pirates, killer whales, icebergs and some truly dreadful cruise-ship singers in her time. But she had never had to deal with fake hair and beauty ladies.

"Right then," she said, straightening her cuffs. "You there." She pointed at Cassie. "Show me that newspaper."

"I promise you it's the truth," Cassie said, handing the paper to Captain Steel. "The women working in the Extremely Elegant Hair and Beauty Salon are imposters."

Cassie's mum bustled forward and grabbed Cassie's hand. "I'm her mother," she said, "and I've no idea what she's talking about. I'm afraid she does make up the silliest stories sometimes—"

"That's enough, thank you!" Captain Steel said suddenly. She wished she was back in her cabin reading a nice book or dealing with something simple, like pirates or icebergs – not listening to some ridiculous story about kidnapping and people locked in storerooms.

"I say, hang on a minute," said Lord Spewitt. He got up from his chair and went over, twiddling his moustache in a thoughtful way. "I recall seeing that very story in the paper just before we sailed. Couple of dastardly dinner ladies…"

"Yes," Cassie said eagerly. "Exactly! They were in Grimguts high-security prison and they escaped the day before the ship sailed!"

"Hmm," Lord Spewitt looked at the newspaper. "Yes, they are a nasty-looking pair. Are you quite sure they're on the ship?"

"They are, honest!" Cassie hopped from one foot to the other impatiently. "Ask these ladies – they're the real hair and beauty staff!" She pulled Poppy and Pippy towards the captain.

Captain Steel looked at Poppy and Pippy. "Is this true?" she asked them. "You've been locked up by two women who took your place on the ship?"

"Yes, it *is* true!" cried Poppy. "We were tied up and thrown in a horrid storeroom by a tall thin woman and a short round woman!"

"And they smelled absolutely vile," said Pippy. Her eyes filled with tears.

"They practically starved us to death!" added Poppy.

Cassie glanced at Captain Steel. "See? It's true. Please come with me right now. Let's find them and you'll see."

20
Miss Crabb and Gladys Goulash's Wigs

"NO!" Rory cried as Miss Crabb dangled Elspeth over the edge of the ship. He rushed towards her, but Miss Crabb gave him a vicious kick to the shins and he hopped back in pain.

Elspeth flailed her arms, scrabbling for something to grab on to, but Miss Crabb was holding her too far out. Elspeth had never been so frightened in her life. She was sure she could see a shark circling in the water below.

"GIVE ME MY RECIPE!" Miss Crabb hollered again.

Just as Elspeth was about to give up and tell her where the recipe was, Gladys Goulash hissed, "Oi! Someone's coming!"

In one swift movement Miss Crabb dragged Elspeth back over the railing and plonked her down on the deck.

"Gah! Get over there," Miss Crabb said, shoving Elspeth and Rory behind a huge lifeboat.

Elspeth gasped for breath, taking in big lungfuls of air. Rory flung an arm around her and they cowered behind the lifeboat.

The door to the deck burst open and Cassie and Captain Steel rushed out, followed by Poppy and Pippy, Cassie's mum and dad, Lord and Lady Spewitt, a confused Tinkiewinks, Petunia and Albert Galoshes-Gallop, Baron Van Der Blink, Jimmy McScoff and a whole load of other passengers.

"There they are!" Cassie shouted, pointing at Miss Crabb and Gladys Goulash.

Miss Crabb grabbed Gladys Goulash and tried to hide behind her. But it didn't work, because Miss Crabb was so much taller than Gladys Goulash.

"We can see you," Captain Steel said firmly. "Come out from behind your friend."

Elspeth and Rory slipped further back into the shadow of the lifeboat as more passengers pushed their way up on deck.

"Come out RIGHT NOW!" Captain Steel shouted.

"What? Why? I ain't done nothing!" shrieked Miss Crabb.

The captain gestured to Jimmy McScoff, who stepped forward and yanked Miss Crabb out from behind Gladys Goulash.

"Well," said Captain Steel. "These ladies certainly look rather like the escaped criminals on the front page of the newspaper … although they do have different hair."

There was a dreadful pause.

Elspeth peeked out from behind the lifeboat and caught Cassie's eye in the crowd. She pointed to her own hair, then pulled a piece of it upwards, hoping Cassie would get the message.

Pull off their wigs! she thought, wishing she could send the idea right into Cassie's head.

It worked. Cassie's eyes widened as she realized what Elspeth was suggesting, and she pushed her way to the front of the crowd.

"Do you recognize them NOW?" asked Cassie. She jumped up, pulling off Miss Crabb's wig with one hand and Gladys Goulash's wig with the other.

Miss Crabb screeched and tried to bite
Cassie and Gladys gave a nervous burp.

"Yes! The very same ladies from the
newspaper!" Lord Spewitt cried. "Gosh,
without those wigs it's quite obvious." He
took a step backwards. "The … smell …

is also quite unpleasant. I believe that was mentioned in the article, too."

"I'll radio to shore immediately," said Captain Steel. "Jimmy McScoff, would you kindly keep these ladies captive in the bin store. Once all the passengers have disembarked, we can hand them over to the authorities."

"Aye, aye, Cap'n," said Jimmy McScoff. "I never was very happy with that hairstyle they gave me."

Elspeth and Rory looked at each other in delight as Miss Crabb and Gladys Goulash were hauled away, kicking and spitting and struggling and shouting.

When the stream of curious passengers had left the deck, Elspeth and Rory fled back to their cabin. They were safe once more – and, even better, they had the recipe.

21
Safe Once More

"Elspeth, you did it!" Rory jumped up and down on his bed with glee. Lazlo jumped on the pillow, making smaller bounces. "Oh, I thought it was the end of you when she dangled you over the edge! But we're safe from Crabb and Goulash again *and* you've got your recipe back!"

Elspeth took a run across the room and

jumped up on to the bed with him, and they held hands and bounced together. She was so relieved that she didn't know what to say.

They heard Cassie's special knock at the door.

"Oh my goodness!" Cassie cried, dancing in and hugging first Elspeth, then Rory. "That was so exciting! And you should see what they've done to Miss Crabb and Gladys Goulash. That bin room smells almost as bad as they do!"

Elspeth started laughing. "You were brilliant! Thanks, Cassie," she said. "We couldn't have done it without you."

"No, you're the one who came up with all the clever ideas!" said Cassie. "But what now? How are you going to get back to England?"

"I'm going to have to confess to Tunnock that I'm here," Rory said, feeding Lazlo their very last bit of chocolate. "Then he can come and collect me."

"Won't your parents come and get you?" Cassie asked.

"Oh no. Hopefully they won't even know I've been gone," Rory said. "Tunners won't tell them. He'll be worried about getting into trouble. But I doubt he'll let me out of his sight ever again! He'll go absolutely bonkers when I tell him where I am."

Rory picked up the cabin phone, punched in a number and waited.

Elspeth could hear a high-pitched shriek on the other end of the phone when Rory explained where he was, then a lot of questions. Rory had been right – Mr Tunnock had gone absolutely bonkers.

Elspeth listened as Rory tried to convince Tunnock he was about to arrive in New York, then tried to convince Tunnock to stop weeping, then tried to convince Tunnock to fly the private jet over to meet them. Eventually he put the phone down.

"Well," he said. "Tunners is pretty upset with me, but he's on his way. He's contacting the head butler at the International Grand Hotel, who will meet us when the ship docks. He'll look after us until Tunners arrives."

"Thank goodness!" Elspeth squeezed his arm. "Good work, Rory. I didn't fancy having to stow away on another ship to get back home."

"But you would have done it if you had to," Rory said. "And you would have managed, Elspeth, because you're brave like that."

Then he looked embarrassed and went a bit pink. "Anyway it's time to pack our things," he said, picking up his satchel.

Down in the stinky bin room, Miss Crabb was stomping around in a rage, kicking over stacks of empty cardboard boxes. Gladys Goulash had settled herself down next to a tub full of old vegetable peelings and was munching on some carrot skins.

"Mmm, not bad, these," she said, picking a piece of carrot out of her teeth. "Quite tasty."

"Gah!" Miss Crabb shuddered with rage and marched towards Gladys, but she slipped on an old banana skin and landed on her back with her feet in the air. As you can imagine, dear reader, this did not improve her mood.

"Stupid banana skin … idiot child … my plan's been RUINED!" Miss Crabb cried as she hauled herself upright. She started kicking the door in a fit of rage.

Jimmy McScoff gave the door a thump from the outside and Miss Crabb jumped backwards.

"Put a sock in it, woman!" he yelled. "I've got a fish slice out here and I'm not afraid to use it!"

Miss Crabb grumbled to herself, but she sat down next to Gladys and stared at the door through narrowed eyes.

"You haven't seen the last of me, Elspeth Hart," she muttered.

22

The Very Last Sighting
of Miss Crabb

On the final morning of the *HMS
Unsinkable*'s voyage, Elspeth woke up early
and lay for a long time, thinking about
her mum and dad as the ship ploughed on
through the waves.

Are you really in Australia? she wondered.
She thought about how worried they must
be. *I'm going to find you, Mum and Dad,*

she thought. She concentrated as hard as she could, trying to make her thoughts zip across the world to wherever her parents were. *The recipe is safe at last and I'm going to find you.*

Just then, a loud voice came over the tannoy. "Lords, ladies and gentlemen! We hope you have had a wonderful time on the *HMS Unsinkable*. Please be advised that we dock in New York in fifteen minutes."

"This is it, Elspeth," Rory said, jumping out of bed. "We're almost there! Can you see any land yet?"

They both peered out of the porthole and spotted a long, hazy line of coast in the distance. Then they heard Cassie's special knock at the door.

"I can't stop," Cassie said, rushing in. "I just wanted to give you this. It's my mum's old golfing umbrella. It's huge. You can put it up when you're leaving and slip through the crowd. The weather forecast says rain, so everyone will have umbrellas, and they won't notice another…" Cassie gave a little hiccup and swiped at her eyes.

"Cassie, are you crying?" Rory asked.

"No!" said Cassie indignantly. "I never cry! Crying's for babies!" But she dashed across the room and hugged first Rory, then Elspeth. Then she patted Lazlo on the head and for once he didn't try to bite or wriggle away.

"I'll write to you both," Cassie said. Then she sniffed and wiped at her eyes again. "Can't stay," she added, and hurried out.

Elspeth and Rory smiled at each other.

"Looks like Cassie's not very good at goodbyes," said Rory.

"Maybe she's not as tough as she makes out," Elspeth said. "I hope we meet her again one day."

Elspeth felt as though she was in a dream as they followed the stream of passengers getting off the ship. Nobody paid any attention to them, because they were all too busy talking about what an exciting voyage it had been.

"I can't imagine I shall EVER be able to eat another meal after all that drama!" Petunia was saying loudly as she moved down the gangway with Albert.

"Yes, dear," said Albert.

"I quite agree," said Lady Spewitt. She was holding Tinkiewinks, who was dressed in a sailor costume.

"I'm thinking of writing a book about it," said Lady Spewitt. "It will be called *Our Terror on the Seas*, and Tinkiewinks will help me write it!"

Tinkiewinks howled and tried to scratch her, but Lady Spewitt gave a dainty laugh and pretended she hadn't noticed.

The rain was hammering on Elspeth and Rory's umbrella, and they had to make their way carefully down the slippery gangway. Elspeth could just make out some people on the docks. One of them was a man in a smart uniform holding a sign that read *Guests of Mr Tunnock*.

"Master Rory! I have been expecting you and your friend!" The butler swept towards them, taking their bags and drawing them towards a taxi.

He was nothing like Mr Tunnock. He

was short and plump and smiley.

"I shall settle you comfortably in my hotel until your Mr Tunnock collects you. He has instructed me not to let you out of my sight!"

"I told you it'd all be fine," Rory said to Elspeth as they clambered into the taxi. "I was never really that worried about any of it."

Elspeth knew that wasn't quite true, but she smiled and didn't say anything. She didn't dare to think how things would have turned out without Rory to help her.

As they drove off, Elspeth gazed back at the *HMS Unsinkable*, enjoying the sound of the rain drumming on the roof of the taxi. She touched the top of her trainer and felt the folded-up recipe there. She'd done it. The recipe was safe once more.

And then something caught her eye.

At the side of the *HMS Unsinkable*, she spotted a small splash as a little boat hit the water. It looked as though someone was rowing away in one of the lifeboats.

Elspeth strained her eyes to see better. Yes, someone *was* rowing away in one of the lifeboats. In fact, there were two people. It looked as though one very tall person and one short dumpy person were rowing away as fast as they possibly could.

Elspeth gulped.

It *couldn't* be … could it?

Where will Elspeth go now?

Find out in her
next adventure...
COMING SOON!

Read how it all began...

Sarah Forbes

Elspeth Hart
and the
School for Show-offs

OUT NOW!

Hart's Extra-special Sticky Toffee Sauce

One is for sugar
Two is for butter
Three is for syrup
Four is for vanilla
Five is for treacle
Six is for cream

Melt it all in till it tastes like a dream!

1=55

2=55

3=1

6=200

5=1

4=0.5

You can find the Extra-special Sticky Toffee Sauce recipe
and much more on my website!
www.elspethhart.com